for Regina
—H.Z.

for Janvier
—G.M.

VIKING
Published by the Penguin Group
Penguin Putnam Books for Young Readers, 345 Hudson Street, New York, New York 10014, U.S.A.
Penguin Books Ltd, 27 Wrights Lane, London W8 5TZ, England
Penguin Books Australia Ltd, Ringwood, Victoria, Australia
Penguin Books Canada Ltd, 10 Alcorn Avenue, Toronto, Ontario, Canada M4V 3B2
Penguin Books (N.Z.) Ltd, 182-190 Wairau Road, Auckland 10, New Zealand

Penguin Books Ltd, Registered Offices: Harmondsworth, Middlesex, England

First published in 2000 by Viking, a division of Penguin Putnam Books for Young Readers.

10 9 8 7 6 5 4 3 2 1

LIBRARY OF CONGRESS CATALOGING-IN-PUBLICATION DATA
Ziefert, Harriet.
Hats off for the Fourth of July! / Harriet Ziefert ; illustrated by Gustaf Miller.
Summary: Spectators wait to see what will come next as they watch the town's Fourth of July parade
ISBN 0-670-89118-5
[1.Parades—Fiction. 2. Fourth of July—Fiction. 3. Stories in rhyme.] I. Miller, Gustaf, ill. II. Title.
PZ8.3.Z47 Hat 2000 [E]—dc21 99-042057

Printed in China
Set in OptiAdrift

HATS Off
for the
Fourth of July!

★

by Harriet Ziefert

illustrated by Gustaf Miller

★

VIKING

In Chatham town on the Fourth of July,
A grand parade will go marching by.

Music and drum ... music and drum.
We're all waiting to see it come.

The twirlers are walking down the street.
They spin and strut and lift their feet.

Music and drum ... music and drum.
Who will be the next to come?

Cowboys on horses yell out loud.
We all shout back—what a happy crowd.

Music and drum ... music and drum.
Who will be the next to come?

The big kids sit on top of the whale.
I'll ride next year right near his tail.

Music and drum ... music and drum.
Miss Eelgrass will be the next to come.

She's the favorite of Chatham town.
Her hair is green and wraps around.

Music and boom ... music and boom!
The big bass drum should be coming soon.

The high school band proudly marches by.

What a sunny day! What a bright blue sky!

Music and vroom. Music and vroom!

The motorcycles need plenty of room.

Patriots march with their muskets and hats.

The Little League follows with baseball bats.

Everyone marches on the Fourth of July.

Hats off!
The flag is passing by!

Music and drum . . . music and drum.

We're sorry that the end has come.

The parade is over, but look in the sky.
Hooray for us all on the Fourth of July!